To Ryan, for coming over that night. —K.L.

To Sami and Amina, always. —N.A.

Text copyright © 2023 by Kyle Lukoff • Illustrations copyright © 2023 by Nadia Alam • All rights reserved. Published by Orchard Books, an imprint of Scholastic Inc., *Publishers since 1920.* ORCHARD BOOKS and design are registered trademarks of Watts Publishing Group, Ltd., used under license. SCHOLASTIC and associated logos are trademarks and/or registered trademarks of Scholastic Inc. • The publisher does not have any control over and does not assume any responsibility for author or third-party websites or their content. • No part of this publication may be reproduced, stored in a retrieval system, or transmitted in any form or by any means, electronic, mechanical, photocopying, recording, or otherwise, without written permission of the publisher. For information regarding permission, write to Scholastic Inc., Attention: Permissions Department, 557 Broadway, New York, NY 10012 • This book is a work of fiction. Names, characters, places, and incidents are either the product of the author's imagination or are used fictitiously, and any resemblance to actual persons, living or dead, business establishments, events, or locales is entirely coincidental. • Library of Congress Cataloging-in Publication Data Available • ISBN 978-1-338-77621-8 • 10 9 8 7 6 5 4 3 2 1   23 24 25 26 27 • Printed in China   38 • First printing, May 2023 Nadia Alams's art was created by digital painting in Procreate and Photoshop. The text type was set in Baskerville Hand Drawn created by Nadia Alam • Designed by Rae Crawford

AWAKE, ASLEEP

by KYLE LUKOFF • illustrations by NADIA ALAM

ORCHARD BOOKS
New York
An imprint of Scholastic Inc.

A kiss, a blink, a dawn,

a break.

A yawn,

a peep,

a stretch,

awake!

A sniff, a stink, a change,

a drink.

A play, a block,

a dress, a pink.

A shoe, a walk,

a laugh, a talk.

A grab,

a land,

a slow,

a stalk.

A reach,

a hand,

a rise,

a stand.

A sun, a clap, a dig, a sand.

A poke,

a snap,

a tear,

a lap.

A try, a fall,

a crash, a nap.

A take, a pry, a scream, a cry.

A touch, a look, a wet, a dry.

A chair, a nook, a wait, a cook.

A hold, a keep, a voice, a book.

A yawn,

a peep,

a stretch,

a heap.

A kiss, a blink, a night,

asleep.